17538

A Treasury of
NURSERY
RHYMES

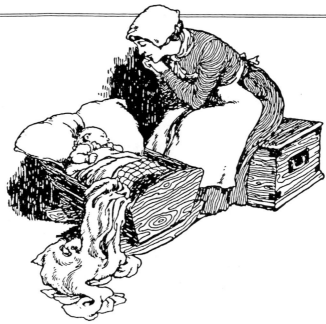

A Treasury of
NURSERY RHYMES

With Classic Illustrations
Edited by Michael Foss
Designed by Martin Bristow

MICHAEL O'MARA BOOKS LIMITED

First published in Great Britain by
Michael O'Mara Books Ltd
20 Queen Anne Street
London W1N 9FB

ISBN: 0 948397 00 4

Picture Research: Mary Corcoran

Printed in Spain by Graficas Estella, Navarra

Contents

Introduction

In Boston, Massachusetts, in the late 17th century, there was said to be a formidable goodwife by the name of Mistress Elizabeth Goose. In her time sixteen children had clung to her skirts, a noisy little army which she soothed and entertained with a stream of nursery rhymes drawn up from her voluminous memory. Her son-in-law, doubly impressed by the depth of her memory and by the joyful effects of the rhymes on the children, set them down and called the book *Mother Goose's Melodies for Children*. Alas, this story is an invention, put about in the 19th century to give a local home and explanation to a more international character: the Boston housewife was in reality the American personification of the old German *Fru Gosen*, the French *Mère Oye* and the English *Mother Goose*.

But this pleasant little American tale is a sign that 'Mother Goose' with her store of children's verse is a substantial, even a necessary figure in the childhood of all nations. She had been around for so long and had fitted so comfortably into tradition, all countries were convinced they owned her. In fact, 'Mother Goose' is every mother (and father too!) of every child everywhere. She is the fond nurse who calms, delights, instructs and corrects her child with a happy and varied body of verse which has proved so powerful and effective that it is repeated and extended in every generation. Here, then, is a collection for our age.

But what *is* a nursery rhyme? We are accustomed to think of it as one of the simple verses that appeared in the many early volumes of *Mother Goose*. We now know, however, that the rhymes for those books were drawn from a thousand different sources – from plays, chap-books, broadsheets, moral pamphlets, popular songs, as well as from oral tradition; and the works of poets everywhere, alive and dead, were not neglected. Indeed, we may say that a nursery rhyme is nothing more or less than a verse, from whatever source, that enters into the particular imaginative world of the child. In this world, reality is insecure and changeable, things are seen simple and stark, the colours are bold, joy and terror are not far apart, and nonsense is just as good as sense. It is a world into which an old blind fiddler may enter as easily as a Shakespeare.

The rhymes in this book – verses as various and divergent as those that made up the original *Mother Goose* – are the ancient and modern poetry of the child's world.

Beginnings

Sleep, baby, sleep,
Thy father guards the sheep;
Thy mother shakes the dreamland tree
And from it fall sweet dreams for thee,
Sleep, baby, sleep.

I'm so sorry for old Adam,
  Just as sorry as can be;
For he never had no mammy
  For to hold him on her knee.

For he never had no childhood,
  Playin' round the cabin door,
And he never had no daddy
  For to tell him all he know.

And I've always had the feelin'
  He'd a let that apple be,
If he'd only had a mammy
  For to hold him on her knee.

We dance round in a ring and suppose,
But the Secret sits in the middle and knows.

What is there hid in the heart of a rose,
      Mother-mine?
Ah, who knows, who knows, who knows?
A Man that died on a lonely hill
May tell you, perhaps, but none other will,
      Little child.

What does it take to make a rose,
      Mother-mine?
The God that died to make it knows
It takes the world's eternal wars,
It takes the moon and all the stars,
It takes the might of heaven and hell
And the everlasting Love as well,
      Little child.

I'm goin' away for to stay a little while,
But I'm comin' back if I go ten thousand miles.
Oh, who will tie your shoes?
And who will glove your hands?
And who will kiss your ruby lips when I am gone?

Oh, it's pappy'll tie my shoes,
And mammy'll glove my hands,
And you will kiss my ruby lips when you come back!

Oh, he's gone, he's gone away,
For to stay a little while,
But he's comin' back if he goes ten thousand miles.

Chicken in the bread-pan,
Pickin' up the dough;
Granny will your dog bite?
No, child, no.

All I need to make me happy,
Two little boys to call me pappy,
One named Biscuit t'other named Gravy,
If I had another I'd call him Davy.

There was an Old Woman
Lived under a hill,
And if she isn't gone
She lives there still.

Baked apples she sold
And cranberry pies,
And she's the old woman
That never told lies.

Young lambs to sell.
Young lambs to sell.
If I'd as much money as I can tell,
I never would cry – Young lambs to sell.

London Bridge is falling down,
Falling down, falling down,
London Bridge is falling down,
My fair lady.

Build it up with wood and clay,
Wood and clay, wood and clay,
Build it up with wood and clay,
My fair lady.

Build it up with bricks and mortar,
Bricks and mortar, bricks and mortar,
Build it up with bricks and mortar,
My fair lady.

Bricks and mortar will not stay,
Will not stay, will not stay,
Bricks and mortar will not stay,
My fair lady.

Build it up with iron and steel,
Iron and steel, iron and steel,
Build it up with iron and steel,
My fair lady.

Iron and steel will bend and bow,
Bend and bow, bend and bow,
Iron and steel will bend and bow,
My fair lady.

Build it up with silver and gold,
Silver and gold, silver and gold,
Build it up with silver and gold,
My fair lady.

Silver and gold will be stolen away,
Stolen away, stolen away,
Silver and gold will be stolen away,
My fair lady.

Set a man to watch all night,
Watch all night, watch all night,
Set a man to watch all night,
My fair lady.

Suppose the man should fall asleep,
Fall asleep, fall asleep,
Suppose the man should fall asleep,
My fair lady.

Give him a pipe to smoke all night,
Smoke all night, smoke all night,
Give him a pipe to smoke all night,
My fair lady.

I brought my love a cherry that has no stone,
I brought my love a chicken that has no bone,
I told my love a story that has no end,
I brought my love a baby and no crying.

How can there be a cherry that has no stone?
How can there be a chicken that has no bone?
How can there be a story that has no end?
How can there be a baby and no crying?

A cherry when it's blooming, it has no stone;
A chicken in the egg, it has no bone;
The story of our love shall have no end;
A baby when it's sleeping does no crying.

Three children sliding on the ice,
   Upon a summer's day,
As it fell out, they all fell in,
   The rest they ran away.

Now had these children been at home,
   Or sliding on dry ground,
Ten thousand pounds to one penny
   They had not all been drowned.

You parents all that children have,
   And you that have got none,
If you would have them safe abroad,
   Pray keep them safe at home.

A tumbled down, and hurt his Arm, against a bit of wood.

B said, 'My Boy, O! do not cry; it cannot do you good!'

C said, 'A Cup of Coffee hot can't do you any harm.'

D said, 'A Doctor should be fetched, and he would cure the arm.'

E said, 'An Egg beat up with milk would quickly make him feel well.'

F said, 'A Fish, if broiled, might cure, if only by the smell.'

G said, 'Green Gooseberry fool, the best of cures I hold.'

H said, 'His Hat should be kept on, to keep him from the cold.'

I said, 'Some Ice upon his head will make him better soon.'

J said, 'Some Jam, if spread on bread, or given in a spoon!'

K said, 'A Kangaroo is here, – this picture let him see.'

L said, 'A Lamp pray keep alight, to make some barley tea.'

M said, 'A Mulberry or two might give him satisfaction.'

N said, 'Some Nuts, if rolled about, might be a slight attraction.'

O said, 'An Owl might make him laugh, if only it would wink.'

P said, 'Some Poetry might be read aloud, to make him think.'

Q said, 'A Quince I recommend, – a Quince, or else a Quail.'

R said, 'Some Rats might make him move, if fastened by their tail.'

S said, 'A Song should now be sung, in hopes to make him laugh!'

T said, 'A Turnip might avail, if sliced or cut in half!'

U said, 'An Urn, with water hot, placed underneath his chin.'

V said, 'I'll stand upon a chair, and play a Violin.

W said, 'Some Whisky-Whizzgigs fetch, some marbles and a ball!'

X said, 'Some double XX ale would be the best of all.'

Y said, 'Some Yeast mixed up with salt would make a perfect plaster!'

Z said, 'Here is a box of Zinc! Get in, my little master!

'We'll shut you up! We'll nail you down! We will, my little master!

'We think we've all heard quite enough of this your sad disaster!'

23

Ring-a-ring o' roses,
A pocket full of posies,
A-tishoo, a-tishoo!
We all fall down.

Hickory, dickory, dock,
The mouse ran up the clock.
The clock struck one,
The mouse ran down,
Hickory, dickory, dock

Baa, baa, black sheep
Have you any wool?
Yes sir, yes sir,
Three bags full;
One for the master,
And one for the dame,
And one for the little boy
Who lives down the lane.

Girls are dandy,
Made of candy:
That's what little girls are made of.
Boys are rotten,
Made of cotton:
That's what little boys are made of.

Flies in the buttermilk, two by two,
If you can't get a red-bird, a blue-bird'll do.
I've lost my girl, now what'll I do?
I'll get another, a better one too.
Pa's got a shotgun, Number 32.
Hurry up slowpoke, do, do, do.
My little girl wears a No 9 shoe,
When I go a-courting, I take two.
Gone again, now what'll I do?
I'll get another, sweeter than you.
He's got big feet, and awkward too.
Kitten in the haymow, mew, mew, mew.
I'll get her back in spite of you.
We'll keep it up 'til half past two.
One old boot and a rundown shoe.
Stole my partner, skip to my Lou.
Skip to my Lou, skip to my Lou,
Skip to my Lou, my darling.

Little Jack Horner
Sat in the corner,
Eating a Christmas pie;
He put in a thumb,
And pulled out a plum,
And said, What a good boy am I.

ALICE WANKE

BAA, BAA! BLACK SHEEP

Beasts and
Other Animals

Massah had an old black mule,
His name was Simon Slick,
The only mule with screamin' eyes,
An' how that mule could kick.

He kicked the feathers from the goose,
He broke the elephant's back,
He stopped the Texas railroad train
An' he kicked it off the track.

The Lord made an elephant,
He made him stout;
The first thing he made
Was the elephant's snout.

He made his snout nigh long as a rail,
The next thing he made was the elephant's tail;
He made his tail to fan the flies,
The next thing he made was the elephant's eyes.

He made his eyes to see green trees,
The next thing he made was the elephant's knees.
Oh, elephant, you shall be free,
Oh, elephant, you shall be free,
When the good Lord sets you free.

Five little monkeys walked along the shore;
One went a-sailing,
Then there were four.
Four little monkeys climbed up a tree;
One of them tumbled down,
Then there were three.
Three little monkeys found a pot of glue;
One got stuck in it,
Then there were two.
Two little monkeys found a currant bun;
One ran away with it,
Then there was one.
One little monkey cried all afternoon,
So they put him in an aeroplane
And sent him to the moon.

I dreamed that my horse had wings and could fly,
I jumped on my horse and rode to the sky.
The man in the moon was out that night,
He laughed long and loud when I pranced into sight.

My Mammy was a wall-eyed goat,
My Old Man was an ass,
I feed myself off leather boots
And dynamite and grass.
For I'm a mule, a long-eared fool
And I ain't never been to school
    Hee-hee-haw.

Three mice went into a hole to spin,
Puss passed by and she peeped in:
'What are you doing, my little men?'
'Weaving coats for gentlemen.'
'Please let me come in to wind off your thread.'
'Oh no, Mistress Pussy, you'll bite off our heads.'

Says Puss: 'You look so wondrous wise,
I like your whiskers and bright black eyes,
Your house is the nicest house I see,
I think there is room for you and me.'
The mice were so pleased that they opened the door,
And pussy soon laid them all dead on the floor.

I WISH I were a
Elephantiaphus
And I could pick off the coconuts with my nose.
But, oh! I am not,
(Alas! I cannot be)
An Elephanti-
Elephantiaphus.
But I'm a cockroach
And I'm a water-bug,
I can crawl around and hide behind the sink.

I wish I were a
Rhinoscereeacus
And could wear an ivory toothpick in my nose.
But, oh! I am not,
(Alas, I cannot be)
A Rhinoscori-
Rhinoscereeacus.
But I'm a beetle
And I'm a pumpkin-bug,
I can buzz and bang my head against the wall.

I wish I were a
Hippopopopotamus
And could swim the Tigris and broad Gangés.
But, oh! I am not,
(Alas! I cannot be)
A hippopopo-
Hippopopopotamus.
But I'm a grasshopper
And I'm a katydid,
I can play the fiddle with my left hind-leg.

I wish I were a
Levileviathan
And had seven hundred knuckles in my spine.
But, oh! I am not,
(Alas! I cannot be)
A Levi-ikey-
A Levi-ikey-mo.
But I'm a firefly
And I'm a lightning-bug,
I can light cheroots and gaspers with my tail.

'Who's that tickling my back?' said the wall.
'Me,' said a small
Caterpillar. 'I'm learning
To crawl.'

The panther is like a leopard,
Except it hasn't been peppered.
Should you behold a panther crouch,
Prepare to say Ouch.
Better yet, if called by a panther,
Don't anther.

A hungry fox one day did spy,
Some nice ripe grapes that hung so high,
And as they hung they seemed to say
To him who underneath did stay,
'If you can fetch me down you may.'

The fox his patience nearly lost,
With expectations baulked and crossed,
He licked his lips for near an hour,
Till he found the prize beyond his power,
Then he went, and swore the grapes were sour!

There was a little turtle.
He lived in a box.
He swam in a puddle.
He climbed on the rocks.

He snapped at a mosquito
He snapped at a flea.
He snapped at a minnow.
And he snapped at me.

He caught the mosquito.
He caught the flea.
He caught the minnow.
But he didn't catch me.

Four and twenty tailor lads
Were fighting with a slug,
'Hallo, sirs,' said one of them,
'Just hold him by the lug.'
But the beastie from his shell came out,
And shook his fearsome head,
'Run, run, my tailors bold,
Or we will all be dead.'

My sweetheart's a mule in the mines,
I drive her without reins or lines,
   On the bumper I sit,
   I chew and I spit
All over my sweetheart's behind.

Ol Mr Rabbit
You've got a mighty habit
Of jumping in the garden
And eating all my cabbage.

Daddy shot a bear,
Daddy shot a bear,
Shot him through the keyhole,
And he never touched a hair.

Our dog Fred
Et the bread.

Our dog Dash
Et the hash.

Our dog Pete
Et the meat

Our dog Davy
Et the gravy.

Our dog Toffy
Et the coffee.

Our dog Jake
Et the cake.

Our dog Trip
Et the dip.

And – the worst
From the first, –

Our dog Fido
Et the pie-dough.

Old Mistress McShuttle
Lived in a coal-scuttle
Along with her dog and her cat.
What they ate I can't tell,
But 'tis known very well
That not one of the party was fat.

Old Mistress McShuttle
Scoured out her coal-scuttle
And washed both her dog and her cat.
The cat scratched her nose,
So they both came to hard blows,
And who was the gainer by that?

Little Betty Winkle she had a pig,
It was a little pig and not very big;
When he was alive he lived in clover,
But now he's dead and that's all over.
Johnny Winkle, he sat down and cried,
Betty Winkle, she lay down and died;
So there's an end of one, two and three,
Johnny, Betty and little Piggie Wiggie.

Mister Rabbit, Mister Rabbit, your ears mighty long,
Yes, my Lawd, they're put on wrong.

Mister Rabbit, Mister Rabbit, your coat mighty grey,
Yes, my Lawd, 'twas made that way.

Mister Rabbit, Mister Rabbit, your feet mighty red,
Yes, my Lawd, I'm almost dead.

Mister Rabbit, Mister Rabbit, your tail mighty white,
Yes, my Lawd, I'm a-getting out of sight.

Mister Rabbit, Mister Rabbit, you look mighty thin,
Yes, my Lawd, been cutting through the wind.

Every little soul must shine, shine shine,
Every little soul must shine, shine, shine.

The Kitty-Cat Bird, he sat on a Fence.
Said the Wren, your Song isn't worth 10¢.
You're a Fake, you're a Fraud, you're a Hor-rid Pretense!
   – Said the Wren to the Kitty-Cat Bird.

You've too many tunes, and none of them Good:
I wish you would act like a bird really should,
Or stay by yourself down deep in the wood,
   – Said the Wren to the Kitty-Cat Bird.

You mew like a Cat, you grate like a Jay:
You squeak like a Mouse that's lost in the Hay,
I wouldn't be You for even a day,
   – Said the Wren to the Kitty-Cat Bird.

The Kitty-Cat Bird, he moped and he cried.
Then a real cat came with a Mouth so Wide,
That the Kitty-Cat Bird just hopped inside;
'At last I'm myself!' – and he up and died
   – Did the Kitty – the Kitty-Cat Bird.

You'd better not laugh; and don't say, 'Pooh!'
Until you have thought this Sad Tale through:
Be sure that whatever you are is you
   – Or you'll end like the Kitty-Cat Bird.

My gal don't wear button-up shoes,
Her feet too big for gaiters,
All she's fit for – a dip of snuff
And a yellow yam potato.

My dog died of whoopin cough,
My mule died of distemper,
Me an' my girl can't git along,
She's got a nasty temper.

You go saddle the old grey mare,
And I'll go plow old muley.
I'll make a turn 'fore the sun goes down,
And I'll go back home to Julie.

Takes four wheels to hold a load,
Takes two mules to pull double,
Take me back to Georgia land
And I won't be any trouble.

Once I had an old grey mare,
And her back wore out and her belly bare.

Then I turned her down the creek,
Purpose of a little green grass to eat.

Then I took her darned old tracks,
And I found her in a mudhole flat of her back.

Then I feeling very stout,
Took her by the tail and I hoist her out.

Then I thought it was no sin,
I hoist up my knife and I skinned her skin.

Then I put in some moose,
Purpose of to make my winter shoes.

Then I hung it in the loft,
'Long come a rogue and stoled it off.

Darn the rogue that stoled it off,
Left my toes all out to the frost.

In come de animuls two by two,
Hippopotamus and a kangaroo;
Dem bones gona rise agin.

In come de animuls three by three,
Two big cats and a bumble bee;
Dem bones gona rise agin.

In come de animuls fo' by fo',
Two thru de winder and two thru de do';
Dem bones gona rise agin.

In come de animuls five by five,
Almost dead and hardly alive;
Dem bones gona rise agin.

In come de animuls six by six,
Three wid clubs and three wid sticks;
Dem bones gona rise agin.

In come de animuls seben by seben,
Fo' from Hell and de others from Heaven;
Dem bones gona rise agin.

In come de animuls eight by eight,
Four on time and de others late;
Dem bones gona rise agin.

In come de animuls nine by nine,
Four in front and five behind;
Dem bones gona rise agin.

In come de animuls ten by ten,
Five big roosters and five big hens;
Dem bones gona rise agin.

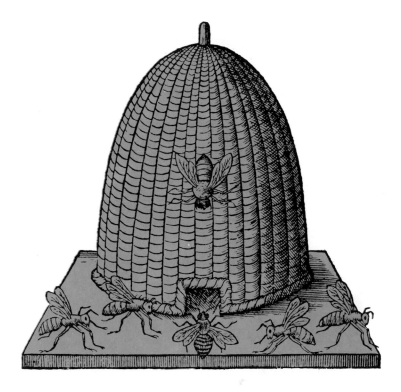

Says the fly, says he, 'Will you marry me,
And live with me, sweet bumble-bee?'

Said the bee, said she, 'I'll live under your wing.
You'll never know I carry a sting.'

So when the parson beetle joined the pair,
They both went out to take the air.

O, the flies did buzz and the bells did ring.
Did you ever hear so merry a thing?

Have Fun !

I never went to college,
I never went to school,
But when it comes to boogie
I'm an educated fool.

I went to the river
And couldn't get across,
Paid five dollars
For an old gray hoss.

The horse wouldn't pull,
So I traded for a bull;

The bull wouldn't holler,
So I traded for a dollar;

The dollar wouldn't pass,
So I throwed it in the grass;

The grass wouldn't grow,
So I traded for a hoe;

The hoe wouldn't dig,
So I traded for a pig;

The pig wouldn't squeal,
So I traded for a wheel;

The wheel wouldn't run,
So I traded for a gun;

The gun wouldn't shoot,
So I traded for a boot;

The boot wouldn't fit,
So I thought I'd better quit.

When I am president of the United States
I'll eat molasses candy and swing on all the gates.

Pussicat, pussicat, with a white foot,
When is your wedding? for I'll come to't.
The beer's to brew, the bread's to bake,
Pussy-cat, pussy-cat, don't be too late.

Girls and boys come out to play,
The moon doth shine as bright as day.
Leave your supper and leave your sleep,
And join your playfellows in the street.
Come with a whoop and come with a call,
Come with good will or not at all.
Up the ladder and down the wall,
A ha-penny loaf will serve us all;
You find milk, and I'll find flour,
And we'll have a pudding in half an hour.

A tisket, a tasket,
Hitler's in his casket;
Eenie, meenie, Mussolini,
Six feet underground.

Hitler, Hitler, I've been thinking,
What in the world have you been drinking?
Smells like beer, tastes like wine;
O my gosh, it's turpentine!

Singing through the forest,
Rattling over ridges,
Shooting under arches,
Running over bridges,
Whizzing through the mountains,
Buzzing o'er the vale,

Bless me! this is pleasant
A-riding on a rail.
Singing through the mountains,
Buzzing o'er the vale,
Bless me! this is pleasant
A-riding on a rail.

I won't be my father's Jack,
I won't be my mother's Jill,
I will be the fiddler's wife,
And have music then I will.

T'other little tune,
T'other little tune,
Prithee, love, play me,
T'other little tune.

Terence McDiddler,
The three-string fiddler,
Can charm, if you please,
The fish from the seas.

Up the hickory,
Down the pine,
Tore my shirt-tail
Way up behind.

I looked down the road,
Saw Sal a-coming,
Thought to my soul
I'd kill myself a-running.

Monkey in the barnyard,
Monkey in the stable,
Monkey git your hair cut
Soon as you are able.

Had a little pony,
His name was Jack.
Put him in a stable,
And he jumped through a crack.

Chew my tobacco,
And spit my juice,
Want to go to heaven,
But it ain't no use.

There was a monkey climbed a tree,
When he fell down, then down fell he.

There was a crow sat on a stone,
When he was gone, then there was none.

There was an old wife did eat an apple,
When she ate two, she ate a couple.

There was a horse going to the mill,
When he went on, he stood not still.

There was a butcher cut his thumb,
When it did bleed, then blood did come.

There was a lackey ran a race,
When he ran fast, he ran apace.

There was a cobbler clouting shoon,
When they were mended, they were done.

There was a navy went to Spain,
When it returned, it came back again.

Ducks in the millpond,
A-geese in the ocean;
A-hug them pretty girls
If I take a notion.

Ducks in the millpond,
A-geese in the clover,
A-jumped in the bed,
And the bed turned over.

Ducks in the millpond,
A-geese in the clover,
A-fell in the millpond,
Wet all over.

My foot in the stirrup, my seat in the saddle,
I'm the best little cowboy that ever rode a-straddle.

I'm on my best horse and I'm going at a run,
I'm the quickest-shooting cowboy that ever pulled a gun.

Oh, my foot's in the stirrup and my hand's on the horn,
I'm the best durn cowboy that ever was born.

With my blankets and my slicker and my rawhide rope,
I'm a-sliding down the trail in a long keen lope.

Oh, a ten-dollar horse and a forty-dollar saddle,
And I'm going to punching Texas cattle.

It's cloudy in the west and looking like rain,
And my darned old slicker's in the wagon again.

I woke up one morning on the old Chisholm Trail
With a rope in my hand and cow by the tail.

My seat in the saddle, and I gave a little shout,
The lead cattle broke and the herd ran about.

I'm up every morning before daylight,
And before I sleep the moon shines bright.

There were three jovial Welshmen, as I have heard them say,
And they would go a-hunting, upon Saint David's day.

All day they hunted and nothing could they find,
But a ship a-sailing, and that they left behind.

One said it was a ship, the other he said 'Nay!'
The third said it was a house with the chimney blown away.

All the night they hunted and nothing could they find,
But the moon a-gliding and that they left behind.

One said it was the moon, the other he said 'Nay!'
The third said it was a cheese with half o't cut away.

And all day they hunted and nothing could they find,
But a hedgehog in a bramble-bush, and that they left behind.

The first said it was a hedgehog, the second he said 'Nay!'
The third said it was a pin-cushion with the pins stuck in wrong way.

And all night they hunted and nothing could they find,
But an owl in a holly tree, and that they left behind.

One said it was an owl, the other he say 'Nay!'
The third said it was an old man, and his beard growing grey.

Dancing Dolly has no sense;
She bought a fiddle for 18 pence.
But the only tune that she could play
Was 'Sally, get out of the Donkey's way'.

Lawd-a-mercy, what have you done?
You've married the old man instead of his son!
His legs are all crooked and wrong put on,
They're all a-laughing at your old man.

Now you're married you must obey.
You must prove true to all you say.
And as you have promised, so now you must do, –
Kiss him twice and hug him, too.

Old Father Long-legs
Can't say his prayers;
Take him by the left leg
And throw him down stairs.
And when he's at the bottom,
Before he long has lain,
Take him by the right leg,
And throw him up again.

Hey diddle diddle,
The cat and the fiddle,
The cow jumped over the moon;
The little dog laughed
To see such sport,
And the dish ran away with the spoon.

This pig went to market;
This pig stayed at home;
This pig had a bit of meat;
And this pig had none;
This pig said, Wee, wee, wee!
I can't find my way home.

Old woman, old woman, will you go a-shearing?
Speak a little louder, sir, I'm rather hard of hearing.
Old woman, old woman, are you good at weaving?
Pray speak a little louder sir, my hearing is deceiving.

Old woman, old woman, will you go a-walking?
Speak a little louder, sir, or what's the good of talking.
Old woman, old woman, are you fond of spinning?
Pray speak a little louder sir, I only see you grinning.

Old woman, old woman, will you do my knitting?
My hearing's getting better now. Come nearer where
  I'm sitting.
Old woman, old woman, shall I kiss you dearly?
O Lawdamercy on my soul, now I hear you clearly!

Humpty Dumpty

Take Heed!

Three blind mice, see how they run!
They all ran after the farmer's wife,
Who cut off their tails with a carving knife,
Did you ever see such a thing in your life,
As three blind mice.

Come, let's to bed, says Sleepy-head;
    Sit up awhile, says Slow.
Hang on the pot, say Greedy Gut,
    We'll sup before we go.

To bed, to bed, cries Sleepy-head,
    But all the rest said, No.
It's morning now, you must milk the cow,
    And tomorrow to bed we go.

Reader, behold! this monster wild
Has gobbled up the infant child.
The infant child is not aware
It has been eaten by the bear.

Tom tied a kettle to the tail of a cat,
Jill put a stone in a blindman's hat,
Bob threw his grandmother down the stairs:
They all grew up ugly, and nobody cares.

A red cockatoo.
Coloured like the peach-tree blossom,
Speaking with the speech of men.
And they did to it what is always done
To the learned and eloquent.
They took a cage with stout bars
And shut it up inside.

I sold me a horse
　　And bought me a cow,
I tried to make bargains
　　But didn't know how.

I sold me a cow
　　And bought me a calf,
I tried to make bargains
　　But always lost half.

I sold me a calf
　　And bought me a swine,
He couldn't chew corn,
　　For his teeth were too fine.

I sold me a swine
　　And bought me a hen,
She laid eggs,
　　But the devil knew when.

I sold me a hen
　　And bought me a cock,
He never crowed
　　Till 9 o'clock.

I sold me a cock
　　And bought me a rat,
His tail caught a-fire,
　　And burned my old hat.

I sold me a rat
　　And bought me a mouse,
His tail caught on fire
　　And burned my old house.

I was standing on the corner
Not doing any harm,
Along came a policeman
And took me by the arm.
He took me round the corner
And rang a little bell,
Along came a police car
And took me to a cell.

I woke in the morning
And looked up on the wall.
The cooties and the bedbugs
Were having a game of ball.
The score was six to nothing,
The bedbugs were ahead.
The cooties hit a home run
And knocked me out of bed.

When the farmer comes to town,
With his wagon broken down,
O, the farmer is the man who feeds them all!
If you'll only look and see,
I think you will agree
That the farmer is the man who feeds them all.

The doctor hangs around
While the blacksmith heats his iron,
O, the farmer is the man who feeds them all!
The preacher and the cook
Go strolling by the brook,
And the farmer is the man who feeds them all.

The farmer is the man,
The farmer is the man,
Buys on credit till the fall.
Tho' his family comes to town,
With a wagon broken down,
O, the farmer is the man who feeds them all!

The rich man lay on his velvet couch,
    He ate from plates of gold;
A poor girl stood on the marble step,
    And cried, 'So cold, so cold!'

Three years went by and the rich man died;
    He descended to fiery hell;
The poor girl lay in an angel's arms
    And sighed, 'All's well – all's well!'

'Twixt Handkerchief and Nose
A difference arose;
And a tradition goes
That they settled it by blows.

I think that I shall never see
A billboard lovely as a tree.
Indeed, unless the billboards fall
I'll never see a tree at all.

The big bee flies high
The little bee makes the honey.
The black folks make the cotton
And the white folks get the money.

Johnny on the railroad, picking up stones,
Along came an engine and broke Johnny's bones.
'O,' said Johnny, 'that's not fair.'
'O,' said the driver, 'I don't care.'

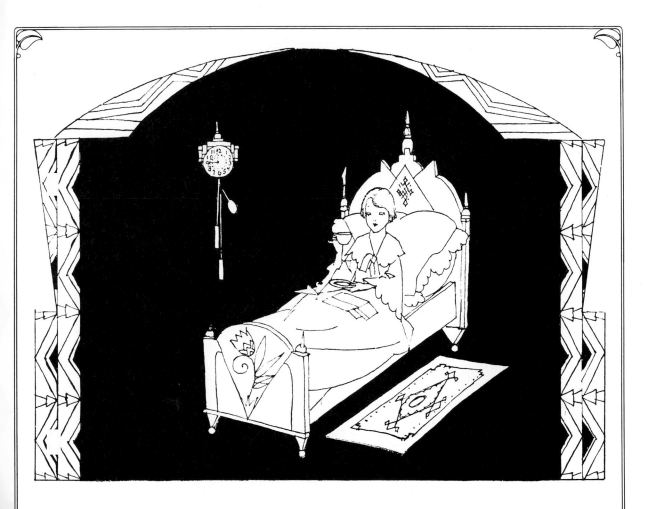

O money is the meat in the cocoanut,
O money is the milk in the jug;
When you've got lots of money
You feel very funny,
You're as happy as a bug in a rug.

My father died a month ago,
He left me all his riches –
A feather bed and a wooden leg,
And a pair of leather breeches;
A coffee pot without a spout,
A cup without a handle,
A baccy box without a lid,
And half a ha'penny candle.

See-saw, Margery Daw.
Jacky shall have a new master;
Jacky shall have but a penny a day,
Because he can't work any faster.

I'll eat when I'm hungry
And drink when I'm dry.
If a tree don't fall on me
I'll live till I die.

There was an old woman who lived in a shoe,
She had so many children she didn't know what to do;
She gave them some broth without any bread;
She whipped them all soundly and put them to bed.

THE OLD WOMAN WHO LIVED IN A SHOE

Step in a hole,
You'll break your mother's sugar bowl.
Step in a crack,
You'll break mother's back.
Step in a ditch,
Your mother's nose will itch.
Step in the dirt,
You'll tear your father's shirt.
Step on a nail,
You'll put your father in jail.

Dr Long is a very good man,
He tries to teach you all he can;
Reading, writing, 'rith-ma-tick,
But he never forgets to use the stick.

Lord Finchley tried to mend the Electric Light
Himself. It struck him dead: And serve him right!
It is the business of the wealthy man
To give employment to the artisan.

Corporal Tim
Was dressed so trim,
He thought them all afraid of him.

But sad to say,
The very first day,
He had a fight,
He died of fright,
And that was the end of Corporal Tim.

Goosey, goosey gander,
Whither shall I wander?
Upstairs and downstairs
And in my lady's chamber.
There I met an old man
Who would not say his prayers.
I took him by the left leg
And threw him down the stairs.

LITTLE TOM TUCKER.

Little Tommy Tucker,
Sings for his supper:
What shall we give him?
White bread and butter.
How shall he cut it
Without a knife?
How will he be married
Without a wife?

My lady Wind, my lady Wind,
Went round about the house to find
A chink to get her foot in.
She tried the keyhole in the door,
She tried the crevice in the floor,
And drove the chimney soot in.

And then one night when it was dark,
She blew up such a tiny spark,
That all the house was pothered.
From it she raised up such a flame,
As flamed away to Belting Lane,
And White Cross folks were smothered.

Mirror, mirror, tell me,
Am I pretty or plain?
Or am I downright ugly
And ugly to remain?

Shall I marry a gentleman?
Shall I marry a clown?
Or shall I marry old knives-and-scissors
Shouting through the town?

Ding, dong bell,
Pussy's in the well!
Who put her in?
Little Tommy Green
Who pulled her out?
Little Johnny Stout.
What a naughty boy was that
To drown poor pussy-cat,
Who never did any harm,
But killed the mice in his father's barn.

The man in the moon
    Came tumbling down,
And asked his way to Norwich;
    He went by the south,
    And burnt his mouth,
With supping cold pease-porridge.

Jack and Jill went up the hill
To fetch a pail of water;
Jack fell down and broke his crown,
And Jill came tumbling after.

Up Jack got, and home did trot,
As fast as he could caper,
To old Dame Dob, who patched his nob
With vinegar and brown paper.

Then Jill came in, and she did grin,
To see Jack's paper plaster;
Her mother whipt her across her knee,
For laughing at Jack's disaster.

Nothing to do but work,
    Nothing to eat but food,
Nothing to wear but clothes
    To keep one from going nude.

Nothing to breathe but air
    Quick as a flash 'tis gone;
Nowhere to fall but off,
    Nowhere to stand but on.

Nothing to comb but hair,
    Nowhere to sleep but in bed,
Nothing to weep but tears,
    Nothing to bury but dead.

Nothing to sing but songs,
    Ah, well, alas! alack!
Nowhere to go but out,
    Nowhere to come but back.

Nothing to see but sights,
    Nothing to quench but thirst,
Nothing to have but what we've got;
    Thus thro' life we are cursed.

Nothing to strike but a gait;
    Everything moves that goes.
Nothing at all but common sense
    Can ever withstand these woes.

Simple Simon.

Simple Simon met a pieman
  Going to the fair;
Says Simple Simon to the pieman,
  'Let me taste your ware.'

Says the pieman to Simple Simon,
  'Show me first your penny.'
Says Simple Simon to the pieman,
  'Indeed I have not any.'

Simple Simon went a-fishing
  For to catch a whale;
All the water he had got
  Was in his mother's pail.

Rain, rain, go away,
Come again another day;
Little Susy wants to play.

As the days grow longer
The storms grow stronger.

Don't cuss the climate
It probably doesn't like you
Any better
Than you like it.

In the garden
Stealing cabbage.
White man's gun,
Rabbit run.
Rabbit stew,
That'll do.

Jack, eating rotten cheese, did say,
Like Samson I my thousands slay:
I vow, quote Roger, so you do,
And with the selfsame weapon too.

Never ask of money spent
Where the spender thinks it went.
Nobody was ever meant
To remember or invent
What he did with every cent.

Liar, liar, lickspit,
Turn about the candlestick,
What's good for liars?
Brimstone and fire.

'Tis Very Strange

There was an old woman tossed up in a basket
   Seventy times as high as the moon;
Where she was going I couldn't but ask it,
   For in her hand she carried a broom.

'Old woman, old woman, old woman,' quoth I,
   'Where are you going to up so high?'
'To brush the cobwebs off the sky!'
   'Shall I go with thee?' 'Aye, by-and-by.'

O what's the weather in a Beard?
It's windy there, and rather weird,
And when you think the sky has cleared
   – Why, there is Dirty Dinky.

Suppose you walk out in a Storm,
With nothing on to keep you warm,
And then step barefoot on a Worm
   – Of course, it's Dirty Dinky.

As I was crossing a hot hot Plain,
I saw a sight that caused me pain,
You asked me before, I'll tell you again:
   – It *looked* like Dirty Dinky.

Last night you lay a-sleeping? No!
The room was thirty-five below;
The sheets and blankets turned to snow.
   – He'd got in: Dirty Dinky.

You'd better watch the things you do.
You'd better watch the things you do.
You're part of him; he's part of you
   – *You* may be Dirty Dinky.

There was a man of Thessaly,
And he was wondrous wise.
He jumped into a bramble bush
And scratched out both his eyes.
And when he saw his eyes were out,
With all his might and main
He jumped into another bush
And scratched them in again.

As I walked by myself
And talked by myself,
Myself said to me,
Look to thyself,
Take care of thyself,
For nobody cares for thee.

One bright morning in the middle of the night,
Two dead boys got up to fight.
Back to back they faced each other,
Drew their swords and shot each other.
Two deaf policemen heard the noise,
Came and shot those two dead boys.
If you don't believe this is true,
Ask the blindman, he saw it too.

Eenie, meenie, minie, mo,
Catchie Castro by the toe.
If he hollers make him say,
'I surrender, USA.'

Annie Mary jumped in the fire;
The fire was too hot, she jumped in the pot;
The pot was too black, she jumped in a crack;
The pot was soon over, she jumped in some clover;
Clover's too sweet, she kicked up her feet;
When her feet were free, she cried 1, 2, 3,
    Then jumped in a tree.
The tree was so high she couldn't go higher,
'Long came a breeze and blew her away.

I had a little husband,
No bigger than my thumb;
I put him in a pint-pot
And there I bade him drum.
I bought a little horse,
That galloped up and down:
I bridled him, and saddled him
And sent him out of town.
I gave him some garters
To garter up his hose,
And a little silk handkerchief
To wipe his pretty nose.

If the wild bowler thinks he bowls,
   Or if the batsman thinks he's bowled,
They know not, poor misguided souls,
   They too shall perish unconsoled.
I am the batsman and the bat
   I am the bowler and the ball,
The umpire, the pavilion cat,
   The roller, pitch, and stumps, and all.

Who are you? A dirty old man,
I've always been since the day I began,
Mother and father were dirty before me,
Hot or cold water has never come o'er me.

If a man who turnips cries
Cry not when his father dies,
Is it not a proof he'd rather
Have a turnip than his father?

There once were two cats of Kilkenny;
Each thought there was one cat too many,
So they fought and they fit,
And they scratched and they bit,
Till, excepting their nails
And the tips of their tails,
Instead of two cats, there weren't any.

Robin the Bobbin, the big-bellied Ben,
He ate more meat than fourscore men;
He ate a cow, he ate a calf,
He ate a butcher and a half,
He ate a church, he ate a steeple,
He ate the priest and all the people.

Rub-a-dub-dub,
Three men in a tub,
And how do you think they got there?
The butcher, the baker,
The candlestick-maker,
They all jumped out of a rotten potato,
'Twas enough to make a man stare.

Got up one morning, went out to plow,
With sixteen oxens and a darned old cow,

Up stepped the old devil sayin', 'How do you do?
There's one in your family that I must have.'

'Oh, please don't take my oldest son,
There's work on the place that's got to be done.'

'It's all I want's that wife of yours.'
'Well, you can have her with all of my heart,
And promise me you'll never depart.'

He picked her up upon his back,
He looked like an eagle skeered off of the rack.

He carried her on about half of the road,
He says, 'Old woman, you're a devil of a load.'

He carried her on to the old devil's door,
There stood a little devil with a ball and chain,
And up with her foot and she kicked out his brains.

Nine little devils went climbing the wall,
Saying, 'Take her back, daddy, she'll murder us all.'

Got up next morning, peeped through the crack,
I spied the old devil come wagging back.

And now you know what a woman can do,
She can whup out the devil and her husband too.

It blew
It snew
It friz
  on
Christmas Day
  so
Merry
They say.

Calico Pie,
The Little Birds fly
Down to the calico tree,
Their wings were blue,
And they sang 'Tilly-loo!'
Till away they flew,
   And they never came back to me!
     They never came back!
     They never came back!
   They never came back to me!

Calico Jam,
The little Fish swam
Over the syllabub sea,
   He took off his hat,
   To the Sole and the Sprat,
   And the Willeby-wat,
But he never came back to me!
   He never came back!
   He never came back!
He never came back to me!

Calico Ban,
The little Mice ran,
To be ready in time for tea,
   Flippity flup,
   They drank it all up,
   And danced in the cup,
But they never came back to me!
   They never came back!
   They never came back!
They never came back to me!

Calico Drum,
The Grasshoppers come,
The Butterfly, Beetle, and Bee,
   Over the ground,
   Around and round,
   With a hop and a bound,
But they never came back to me!
   They never came back!
   They never came back!
They never came back to me!

What's in there?
Gold and money.
Where's my share o't?
The mousie ran awa wi't.
Where's the mousie?
In her housie.
Where's her housie?
In the wood.
Where's the wood?
The fire burnt it.
Where's the fire?

The water quenched it.
Where's the water?
The brown bull drank it.
Where's the brown bull?
Back of Burnie's Hill.
Where's Burnie's Hill?
All clad with snow.
Where's the snow?
The sun melted it.
Where's the sun?
High, high up in the air.

My father he left me three acres of land,
    Sing ivy, sing ivy!
My father he left me three acres of land,
    Sing holly, go whistle and ivy.

I ploughed it one morning with a ram's horn,
    Sing ivy, sing ivy!
And sowed it all over with one pepper corn,
    Sing holly, go whistle and ivy.

I harrowed it next with a bramble bush,
    Sing ivy, sing ivy!
And reaped it all with my little penknife,
    Sing holly, go whistle and ivy.

The mice for me, carried it into the barn,
    Sing ivy, sing ivy!
And there I threshed it with a goose quill,
    Sing holly, go whistle and ivy.

The cat she carried it unto the mill,
    Sing ivy, sing ivy!
And the miller he said that he'd work with a will,
    Sing holly, go whistle and ivy.

O my mother and father were Irish,
And I am Irish too.
O we bought a peck of potatoes,
And they were Irish too.
O we kept a pig in the parlour,
For it was Irish too.

If buttercups buzzed after the bee,
If boats were on land, churches on sea,
If ponies rode men, if grass ate the cows,
And cats should be chased into holes by the mouse,
If mamas sold babies to gypsies for a crown,
If summer were spring and the other way round,
Then all the world would be upside down.

Hic, hoc, the carrion crow,
For I have shot something too low.
I have quite missed my mark,
And shot the poor sow to the heart.
Wife, bring treacle in a spoon,
Or else the poor sow's heart will down.

I'll sing you twelve O
Green grow the rushes O
What are your twelve O?
Twelve for the twelve apostles
Eleven for the eleven that went up to heaven
Ten for the ten commandments
Nine for the nine bright shiners
Eight for the eight bold rainers
Seven for the seven stars in the sky
Six for the six proud walkers
Five for the symbol at your door
Four for the Gospel makers
Three, three for the rivals
Two, two for the lily-white boys
Clothed all in green O
One is one and all alone
And evermore shall be so.

O she looked out of the window,
As white as any milk;
But He looked into the Window,
As black as any silk.

Hallo, hallo, you coalblack smith.
    O what is your silly song?
You never shall change my maiden name
    That I have kept so long.
I'd rather die a maid, yes, but then she said,
    And be buried all in my grave,
Than I'd have such a husky, dusky, fusky, musty
    Coalblack Smith
A maiden I will die.

Then She became a duck,
A duck all on the stream.
And He became a water dog,
And fetched her back again.

Then She became a hare,
A hare all on the plain.
And He became a greyhound dog,
And fetched her back again.

Then She became a fly,
A fly all in the air.
And He became a spider,
And fetched her to his lair.

Hallo, hallo, you coalblack smith.
    O what is your silly song?
You never shall change my maiden name
    That I have kept so long.
I'd rather die a maid, yes, but then she said,
    And be buried all in my grave,
Than I'd have such a husky, dusky, fusky, musty
    Coalblack smith
A maiden I will die.

The Valley of Tears

Call for the robin-redbreast and the wren,
Since o'er shady groves they hover,
And with leaves and flowers do cover
The friendless bodies of unburied men.
Call unto his funeral dole
The ant, the field-mouse, and the mole,
To rear him hillocks that shall keep him warm,
And (when gay tombs are robbed) sustain no harm;
But keep the wolf far thence, that's foe to men,
For with his nails he'll dig them up again.

I saw with open eyes
Singing birds sweet
Sold in the shops
For the people to eat,
Sold in the shops of
Stupidity Street.

I saw in vision
The worm in the wheat,
And in the shops nothing
For people to eat;
Nothing for sale in
Stupidity Street.

'The myrtle bush grew shady
   Down by the ford.'
'Is it even so?' said my lady.
   'Even so!' said my lord.
'The leaves are set too thick together
   For the point of a sword.'

'The arras in your room hangs close,
   No light between!
You wedded one of those
   That see unseen.'
'Is it even so?' said the King's Majesty.
   'Even so!' said the Queen.

IN ONE ANOTHER'S ARMS THEY DYED.

Three little children sitting on the sand,
　　All, all a-lonely,
Three little children sitting on the sand,
　　All, all a-lonely,
Down in the green wood shady.

There came an old woman, said come on with me,
　　All, all a-lonely,
There came an old woman, said come on with me,
　　All, all a-lonely,
Down in the green wood shady.

She stuck her pen-knife through their heart,
　　All, all a-lonely,
She stuck her pen-knife through their heart,
　　All, all a-lonely,
Down in the green wood shady.

There was an old woman and her name was Peg,
Her head was of wood, and she wore a cork leg;
The neighbours all pitched her into the water,
Her leg was drowned first, and her head followed after.

Here lies Fred
Who was alive and is dead.
Had it been his father,
I had much rather;
Had it been his brother,
Still better than another;
Had it been his sister,
No one would have missed her;
Had it been the whole generation,
So much better for the nation;
But since 'tis only Fred
Who was alive and is dead,
Why, there's no more to be said.

When strolling one night mid New York's gay throng,
I met a poor boy, he was singing a song;
Although he was singing, he wanted for bread,
Although he was smiling, he wished himself dead.

Little Bo-peep has lost her sheep,
And can't tell where to find them;
Leave them alone, and they'll come home,
And bring their tails behind them.

Little Bo-peep fell fast asleep,
And dreamt she heard them bleating;
But when she awoke, she found it a joke,
For they were still all fleeting.

Then up she took her little crook,
Determined for to find them;
She found them indeed, but it made her heart bleed,
For they'd left their tails behind them.

It happened one day, as Bo-peep did stray
Into a meadow hard by,
There she espied their tails side by side,
All hung on a tree to dry.

She heaved a sigh, and wiped her eye,
And over the hillocks went rambling,
And tried what she could, as a shepherdess should,
To tack again each to its lambkin.

A man of words and not of deeds
Is like a garden full of weeds;
And when the weeds begin to grow,
It's like a garden full of snow;
And when the snow begins to fall,
It's like a bird upon the wall;
And when the bird away does fly,
It's like an eagle in the sky;
And when the sky begins to roar,
It's like a lion at the door;
And when the door begins to crack,
It's like a stick upon your back;
And when your back begins to smart,
It's like a penknife in your heart;
And when your heart begins to bleed,
You're dead, and dead, and dead indeed.

Humpty Dumpty sat on a wall,
Humpty Dumpty had a great fall.
All the king's horses,
And all the king's men,
Couldn't put Humpty together again.

The north wind doth blow,
And we shall have snow,
And what will poor Robin do then?
Poor thing.
He'll sit in a barn,
And keep himself warm,
And hide his head under his wing.
Poor thing.

A long time ago
I went on a journey,
Right to the corner
Of the Eastern Ocean.
The road there
Was long and winding,
And stormy waves
Barred my path.
What made me
Go this way?
Hunger drove me
Into the World.
I tried hard
To fill my belly:
And even a little
Seemed a lot.
But this was clearly
A bad bargain,
So I went home
And lived in idleness.

Though I am young and cannot tell
Either what Love or Death is well,
Yet I have heard they both bear darts
And both do aim at human hearts.

The wind blows out; the bubble dies;
The spring entombed in autumn lies;
The dew dries up; the star is shot;
The flight is past; and man forgot.

The wind stood up, and gave a shout;
He whistled on his fingers, and

Kicked the withered leaves about,
And thumped the branches with his hand,

And said he'll kill, and kill, and kill;
And so he will! And so he will!

Oh, my liver and my lungs, my lights and my legs,
They're paining me, they're paining me;
My heart is sad, my head is bad,
And I think I'm going crazy.

Crushed by the days of endless toil
And sleepless nights of woe,
There is naught but anguish ev'rywhere
As on through life we go.

He clasps the crag with crooked hands;
Close to the sun in lonely lands,
Ringed with the azure world, he stands.

The wrinkled sea beneath him crawls;
He watches from his mountain walls,
And like a thunderbolt he falls.

Grey as a guinea-fowl is the rain
Squawking down from the boughs again.
 'Anne, Anne,
  Go fill the pail,'
Said the old witch who sat on the rail.
'Though there is a hole in the bucket,
Anne, Anne,
It will fill my pocket;
The water-drops when they cross my doors
Will turn to guineas and gold moidores....'
The well-water hops across the floors;
Whimpering, 'Anne' it cries, implores,
And the guinea-fowl-plumaged rain,
Squawking down from the boughs again,
Cried, 'Anne, Anne, go fill the bucket,
There is a hole in the witch's pocket –
And the water-drops like gold moidores,
Obedient girl, will surely be yours.
So, Anne, Anne,
Go fill the pail
Of the old witch who sits on the rail!'

The Old Woman who
Brushed the Cobwebs off the Sky.

Starlight and Dreams

Pussy-cat, pussy-cat, where have you been?
I've been up to London to look at the queen.
Pussy-cat, pussy-cat, what did you there?
I frighten'd a little mouse under the chair.

Dust always blowing about the town,
Except when sea-fog laid it down,
And I was one of the children told
Some of the blowing dust was gold.

All the dust the winds blew high
Appeared like gold in the sunset sky,
But I was one of the children told
Some of the dust was really gold.

Such was life in the Golden Gate:
Gold dusted all we drank and ate,
And I was one of the children told,
'We all must eat our peck of gold.'

Gipsy in da moonlight,
Gipsy in da dew,
Gipsy never come back,
Before the clock struck two.

Walk in Gipsy, walk in,
Walk right in I say,
Walk into my parlour,
To hear my banjo play.

I don't love nobody,
An' nobody loves me.
All I love is Mary,
To come an' dance with me.

It's nice to get up in the morning when the sun begins to shine,
At four or five or six o'clock in the good old summer time;
But when the snow is snowing, and it's murky overhead,
It's nice to get up in the morning – but nicer to lie in bed.

One evening when the sun was low
And the jungle fires were burning
Down the track came a hobo hamming
And he said, Boys, I'm not turning;
I'm headed for a land that's far away
Beside the crystal fountains.
So come with me, we'll go and see
The Big Rock Candy Mountains.

In the Big Rock Candy Mountains
There's a land that's fair and bright,
Where the handouts grow on bushes
And you sleep out every night.
Where the box-cars all are empty
And the sun shines everyday
On the birds and the bees
And the cigarette trees
The rock-and-rye springs
Where the whangdoodle sings,
In the Big Rock Candy Mountains.

In the Big Rock Candy Mountains
All the cops have wooden legs
And the bulldogs all have rubber teeth
And the hens lay hard-boiled eggs;
The farmers' trees are full of fruit
And the barns are full of hay:
O I'm bound to go
Where there ain't no snow,
And the rain don't fall,
The wind don't blow,
In the Big Rock Candy Mountains.

In the Big Rock Candy Mountains
You never change your socks
And the little streams of alkyhol
Come a-trickling down the rocks;
The shacks all have to top their hats
And the railroad bulls are blind;
There's a lake of stew,
And of whisky too,
You can paddle all around
In a big canoe,
In the Big Rock Candy Mountains.

In the Big Rock Candy Mountains
The jails are made of tin
And you can bust right out again
As soon as they put you in;
There ain't no short-handled shovels,
No axes, saw or picks:
O I'm going to stay
Where you sleep all day,
Where they hung the Turk
That invented work,
In the Big Rock Candy Mountains.
I'll see you all
This coming fall
In the Big Rock Candy Mountains.

This train is bound for glory, this train,
This train is bound for glory, this train,
This train is bound for glory,
If you ride in it, you must be holy, this train.

This train don' pull no extra, this train,
Don' pull nothin' but de Midnight Special.

This train don' pull no sleepers, this train,
Don' pull nothin' but the righteous people, this train.

This train don' pull no jokers, this train,
Neither don' pull no cigar smokers, this train.

This train is bound for glory, this train.
If you ride in it, you mus' be holy, this train.

I had a little nut tree,
Nothing would it bear
But a silver nutmeg
And a golden pear.

The King of Spain's daughter
Came to visit me,
And all for the sake
Of my little nut tree.

I skipped over the ocean,
I danced over the sea,
And all the birds in the air
Couldn't catch me.

Lavender's blue, dilly, dilly,
Lavender's green;
When I am king, dilly, dilly,
You shall be queen.

Call up your men, dilly, dilly,
Set them to work,
Some to the plough, dilly, dilly,
Some to the cart.

Some to make hay, dilly, dilly,
Some to thresh corn,
Whilst you and I, dilly, dilly,
Keep ourselves warm.

Oh! dear! what can the matter be?
Dear! dear! what can the matter be?
Oh! dear! what can the matter be?
Johnny's so long at the fair.

He promised he'd buy me a fairing should please me,
And then for a kiss, oh! he vowed he would tease me,
He promised he'd bring me a bunch of blue ribbons
To tie up my bonny brown hair.

And it's oh! dear! what can the matter be?
Dear! dear! what can the matter be?
Oh! dear! what can the matter be?
Johnny's so long at the fair.

He promised he'd bring me a basket of posies,
A garland of lilies, a garland of roses,
A little straw hat, to set off the blue ribbons
That tie up my bonny brown hair.

And it's oh! dear! what can the matter be?
Dear! dear! what can the matter be?
Oh! dear! what can the matter be?
Johnny's so long at the fair.

Sweet St Lucy let me know,
Whose cloth I shall lay,
Whose bed I shall make,
Whose child I shall bear,
Whose darling I shall be,
Whose arms I shall lie in.

If you can't answer my questions
Oh you're not God's you're one of mine.
And the crow flies over the white oak tree!

Oh what is higher than the tree?
And what is deeper than the sea?
And the crow flies over the white oak tree!

Oh Heaven is higher than a tree,
And Love is deeper than the sea.
And the crow flies over the white oak tree!

Oh what is whiter than the milk?
And what is softer than the silk?

Oh snow is whiter than the milk,
And down is softer than the silk.

Oh what is louder than the horn?
And what is sharper than the thorn?

Oh thunder's louder than the horn,
And hunger's sharper than the thorn.

Oh what is heavier than the lead?
And what is better than the bread?

Oh grief is heavier than the lead.
God's blessing's better than the bread.

Now you have answered my questions nine.
Oh you are God's, you're none of mine.

Mary, Mary, quite contrary,
How does your garden grow?
With silver bells and cockle shells,
And pretty maids all in a row.

Twinkle, twinkle, little star,
How I wonder what you are.
Up above the world so high,
Like a diamond in the sky.

When the blazing sun is gone,
When he nothing shines upon,
Then you show your little light,
Twinkle, twinkle, all the night.

Where are you going, my pretty maid?
  I'm going a-milking, sir, she said.
May I go with you, my pretty maid?
  You're kindly welcome, sir, she said.
What is your father, my pretty maid?
  My father's a farmer, sir, she said.
Say, will you marry me, my pretty maid?
  Yes, if you please, kind sir, she said.
Will you be constant, my pretty maid?
  That I can't promise you, sir, she said.
Then I won't marry you, my pretty maid!
  Nobody asked you, sir! she said.

Ride a cock-horse to Banbury Cross,
To see a fine lady upon a white horse;
Rings on her fingers and bells on her toes,
And she shall have music wherever she goes.

To *my*,
   Ay,
And we'll *furl*,
   Ay,
And pay Paddy Doyle for his boots.

We'll *sing*,
   Ay,
And we'll *heave*,
   Ay,
And pay Paddy Doyle for his boots.

We'll *heave*,
   Ay,
With a *swing*,
   Ay,
And pay Paddy Doyle for his boots.

I know where I'm going,
I know who's going with me,
I know who I love,
But the dear knows who I'll marry.

I'll have stockings of silk,
Shoes of fine green leather,
Combs to buckle my hair
And a ring for every finger.

Feather beds are soft,
Painted rooms are bonny;
But I'd leave them all
To go with my love Johnny.

Some say he's dark,
I say he's bonny,
He's the flower of them all
My handsome, coaxing Johnny.

I know where I'm going,
I know who's going with me,
I know who I love,
But the dear knows who I'll marry.

Over the bleak and barren snow
A voice there came a-calling:
'Where are you going to, Tony O!
Where are you going this morning?'

'I am going where there are rivers of wine,
The mountains bread and honey;
There Kings and Queens do mind the swine,
And the poor have all the money.'

I saw three ships come sailing by,
Come sailing by, come sailing by,
I saw three ships come sailing by
On New Year's Day in the morning.

And what do you think was in them then,
Was in them then, was in them then?
And what do you think was in them then,
On New Year's day in the morning?

Three pretty girls were in them then,
Were in them then, were in them then,
Three pretty girls were in them then,
On New Year's Day in the morning.

One could whistle, and one could sing,
And one could play on the violin;
Such joy there was at my wedding,
On New Year's day in the morning.

I saw a ship a-sailing,
A-sailing on the sea.
And O it was all laden
With pretty things for thee.
There were comfits in the cabin,
And apples in the hold,
And the spreading sails were made of silk
And the masts were made of gold.

The four-and-twenty sailors
That stood between the decks
Were four-and-twenty white mice
With chains about their necks.
The captain was a little duck
With a packet on his back,
And when the ship began to move,
The captain cried Quack, Quack.

I had a boat, and the boat had wings;
    And I did dream that we went a flying
Over the heads of queens and kings,
    Over the souls of dead and dying,
Up among the stars and the great white rings,
    And where the Moon on her back is lying.

Wynken, Blynken and Nod one night
   Sailed off in a wooden shoe –
Sailed on a river of crystal light,
   Into a sea of dew.

'Where are you going, and what do you wish?'
   The old moon asked the three.
'We have come to fish for the herring fish
   That live in this beautiful sea;
   Nets of silver and gold have we!'
       Said Wynken,
       Blynken,
       And Nod.

The old moon laughed and sang a song,
   As they rocked in the wooden shoe,
And the wind that sped them all night long
   Ruffled the waves of dew.
The little stars were the herring fish
   That lived in that beautiful sea –
'Now cast your nets wherever you wish –
   Never afeard are we';
   So cried the stars to the fishermen three:
       Wynken,
       Blynken,
       And Nod.

All night long their nets they threw
   To the stars in the twinkling foam –
Then down from the skies came the wooden shoe,
   Bringing the fishermen home;
'Twas all so pretty a sail it seemed
   As if it could not be,
And some folks thought 'twas a dream they'd dreamed
   Of sailing that beautiful sea –
   But I shall name you the fishermen three:
       Wynken,
       Blynken,
       And Nod.

Wynken and Blynken are two little eyes,
And Nod is a little head,
And the wooden shoe that sailed the skies
  Is a wee one's trundle-bed.

So shut your eyes while mother sings
  Of wonderful sights that be,
And you shall see the beautiful things
  As you rock in the misty sea,
  Where the old shoe rocked the fishermen three:
        Wynken,
        Blynken,
        And Nod.

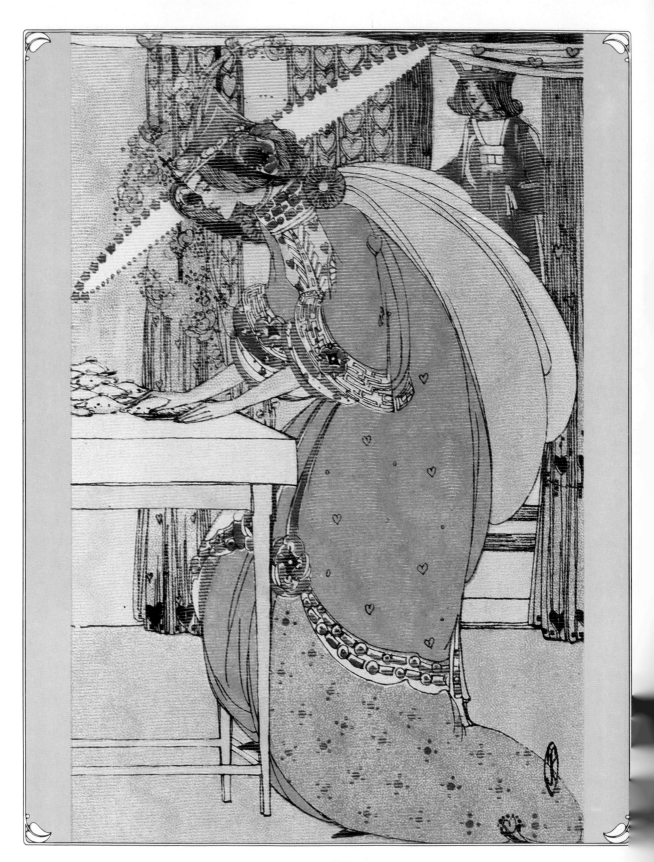

Diminuendo

Fury said to a
mouse, That he
met in the
house,
'Let us
both go to
law: *I* will
prosecute
you. Come,
I'll take no
denial; We
must have a
trial: For
really this
morning I've
nothing
to do.'
Said the
mouse to the
cur, 'Such
a trial,
dear Sir,
With
no jury
or judge,
would be
wasting
our
breath.'
'I'll be
judge, I'll
be jury,'
Said
cunning
old Fury:
'I'll
try the
whole
cause,
and
condemn
you
to
death.'

Fear no more the heat o' the Sun,
Nor the furious Winters rages,
Thou thy worldly task hast done,
Home art gone, and tane thy wages.
Golden Lads and Girls all must,
As Chimney-Sweepers, come to dust.

Fear no more the frown o' th' Great,
Thou art past the Tyrants stroke,
Care no more to clothe, and eat
To thee the Reed is as the Oak:
The Scepter, Learning, Physick must,
All follow this, and come to dust.

Fear no more the Lightning flash,
Nor the all-dreaded Thunder-stone,
Fear not Slander, Censure rash,
Thou has finished joy and moan.
All Lovers young, all Lover must,
Consign to thee, and come to dust. . . .

That so many of the poor should suffer from cold what can we do to prevent?
To bring warmth to a single body is not much use.
I wish I had a big rug ten thousand feet long,
Which at one time could cover up every inch of the City.

Who said, 'Peacock Pie'?
    The old King to the sparrow:
Who said, 'Crops are ripe'?
    Rust to the harrow:

Who said, 'Where sleeps she now?
    Where rests she now her head,
Bathed in eve's loveliness'?
    That's what I said.

Who said, 'Ay, mum's the word';
    Sexton to willow:
Who said, 'Green dusk for dreams,
    Moss for a pillow'?
Who said, 'All Time's delight
    Hath she for narrow bed;
Life's troubled bubble broke'?
    That's what I said.

'Is there anybody there?' said the Traveller,
  Knocking on the moonlit door;
And his horse in the silence champed on the grasses
  Of the forest's ferny floor:
And a bird flew up out of the turret,
  Above the Traveller's head:
And he smote upon the door again a second time;
  'Is there anybody there?' he said.
But no one descended to the Traveller;
  No head from the leaf-fringed sill
Leaned over and looked into his grey eyes,
  Where he stood perplexed and still.
But only a host of phantom listeners
  That dwelt in the lone house then
Stood listening in the quiet of the moonlight
  To that voice from the world of men:
Stood thronging the faint moonbeam on the dark stair,
  That goes down to the empty hall,
Hearkening in an air stirred and shaken
  By the lonely Traveller's call.
And he felt in his heart, their strangeness,
  Their stillness answering his cry,
While his horse moved, cropping the dark turf,
  'Neath the starred and leafy sky;
For he suddenly smote the door, even
  Louder, and lifted his head:
'Tell them I came, and no one answered,
  That I kept my word,' he said.
Never the least stir made the listeners,
  Though every word he spake
Fell echoing through the shadowiness of the still house
  From the one man left awake:
Ay, they heard his foot upon the stirrup,
  And the sound of iron on stone,
And how the silence surged softly backward,
  When the plunging hoofs were gone.

The old dog barks backward without getting up,
I can remember when he was a pup.

The rain to the wind said,
'You push and I'll pelt.'
They so smote the garden bed
That the flowers actually knelt,
And lay lodged – though not dead.
I know how the flowers felt.

When cockle shells turn silver bells,
Then will my love return to me.
When roses blow, in wintry snow,
Then will my love return to me.
Oh, waillie! waillie!
But love is bonnie
A little while when it is new!
But it grows old and waxeth cold,
And fades away like evening dew.

Time to go home!
   Says the great steeple clock.
Time to go home!
   Says the gold weathercock.
Down sinks the sun
   In the valley to sleep;
Lost are the orchards
   In blue shadows deep.
Soft falls the dew
   On cornfield and grass;
Through the dark trees
   The evening airs pass:
Time to go home,
   They murmur and say;
Birds to their home
   Have all flown away.
Nothing shines now
   But the gold weathercock.
Time to go home!
   Says the great steeple clock.

I know moonlight,
I know starlight,
I lay this body down.

I walk in the moonlight,
I walk in the starlight,
I lay this body down.

I go to judgment
In the evenin' of the day,
When I lay this body down.

Wee Willie Winkie runs through the town,
Upstairs and downstairs in his nightgown,
Rapping at the windows, crying through the lock,
Are the children all in bed, for it's gone eight o'clock.

Matthew, Mark, Luke and John,
Bless the bed that I lie on.
Four corners to my bed,
Four angels there be spread.
One to watch and one to pray,
Two to guard my soul always.

God is the branch and I the flower;
Pray God send me a blessed hour.
Now I lay me down to sleep
I give the Lord my soul to keep,
And in the morning when I wake
The Lord's path I shall surely take.

Index of First Lines

Index of Artists

Acknowledgments

The editor and publishers would like to thank the following people for giving permission to include in this anthology material which is in their copyright. The publishers have made every effort to trace copyright holders. If we have inadvertently omitted to acknowledge anyone we should be most grateful if this could be brought to our attention for correction at the earliest opportunity.

George Allen and Unwin for the poems from *Collected Works* by Arthur Waley.
Jonathan Cape Ltd., Holt Rinehart Winston and the author's estate for the poems by Robert Frost.

Constable and Co. Ltd. for the poem by Colin Francis.
Doubleday and Co. Inc. for the poems by Theodore Roethke and Don Marquis.
Duckworth and Co. Ltd. and Alfred A. Knopf Inc for the poem by Hillaire Belloc.
David Higham Associates for the poem by Edith Sitwell.
Little Brown and Co. Inc. for the poems by Ogden Nash.
For the poems of Walter de la Mare, the author's Literary Trustees and the Society of Authors as their representative.
Macmillan London for the poems by Ralph Hodgson and James Stephens.
Oxford University Press for the poem by James Reeves.
Ian Seraillier for his poem.